Too Many Tomatoes

Diane Stango

NEIGHBORHOOD READERS

Rosen Classroom Books & Materials™

New York

I have a tomato plant.

I give the plant lots of water.

Mom and I look at the
tomato plant.
We see tomatoes!

4

I put a tomato on my sandwich.
I put a tomato on Mom's
sandwich, too.

We put tomatoes in the soup.

Look, Mom!
Look at all the tomatoes!

I put tomatoes in a big salad.

Mom helps me make tomato
juice.

Mom helps me make tomato
pie.

Look, Mom!
Look at all the tomatoes!

There are too many tomatoes!